A SCIENCE CHAPTER BOOK

The Magic School Bus

PENGUIN PUZZLE

SCHOLASTIC INC.
New York   Toronto   London   Auckland   Sydney
Mexico City   New Delhi   Hong Kong   Buenos Aires

Written by Judith Bauer Stamper.

Illustrations by Ted Enik.

Based on *The Magic School Bus* books
written by Joanna Cole and illustrated by Bruce Degen.

The author would like to thank Anthony Brownie
for his expert advice in preparing this manuscript.

No part of this publication may be reproduced in whole or in part, or stored in a retrieval system, or transmitted in any form or by any means, electronic, mechanical, photocopying, recording, or otherwise, without written permission of the publisher. For information regarding permission, write to Scholastic Inc., Attention: Permissions Department, 557 Broadway, New York, NY 10012.

ISBN 0-439-20422-4

24 23 22 21 20 19 18 17 16 15 14   3 4 5 6 7 8/0

Designed by Peter Koblish

Printed in the U.S.A.

40

INTRODUCTION

Hi, my name is Phoebe. I am one of the kids in Ms. Frizzle's class.

Maybe you've heard of Ms. Frizzle. (Sometimes we just call her the Friz.) She is a terrific teacher — but a little strange. In fact, things can get really strange in her science class. Science is one of Ms. Frizzle's favorite subjects, and she knows everything about it.

We go on lots of field trips in the Magic School Bus. Believe me, it's not called *magic* for nothing! Once we get on board, anything can happen.

Ms. Frizzle likes to surprise us, but we can usually tell when she is planning a special lesson — we just look at what she is wearing.

One day, the Friz came into class wearing a dress we'd never seen before. That was our first clue — we knew a big trip was on the way. But who could have guessed we'd end up where we did? Even Ms. Frizzle was surprised! Let me tell you what happened when the Magic School Bus went to the bottom of the world!

CHAPTER 1

I ran into Ms. Frizzle's classroom in a big rush. I didn't want to be late that day!

"Phoebe, watch out!" Carlos yelled at me.

I froze in my footsteps. Then I looked up. A big paper eagle was dangling right over my head.

"Yikes!" I screamed.

Carlos was holding on to the eagle by a string. He was trying to hang it from the ceiling. But the eagle was bouncing up and down. It looked as if it wanted to pounce on me and eat me up.

"Wow, Carlos," I said. "That's some bird!"

Carlos, it's giving me the eagle eye!

"It's a bald eagle," Carlos said proudly. "It used to be endangered, but now —"

"But now *we're* in danger," Dorothy Ann interrupted him, joking about the size of Carlos's project.

"Oh, you're just jealous, D.A.," Carlos said. "My eagle is ten times bigger than your robin."

"I'm not jealous," D.A. answered. "I just think all the birds we're studying are amazing."

Just then, Ms. Frizzle came rushing into the room. She ducked in time to miss Carlos's eagle. Its claws just grazed the top of her curly red hair.

"Good morning, class," the Friz said. "I see you all have your bird projects here now. Before you deliver your reports, let's go on a little field trip."

"Uh-oh!" Arnold said. "I think I should've stayed home today."

Every pair of eyes in the room stared at Ms. Frizzle's dress. We had never seen this dress before. It was mostly blue — sky blue — with birds flying all over it.

"Ms. Frizzle," Carlos said, "that dress is for the birds."

We all groaned. We thought Carlos's jokes were for the birds.

"Are we going bird-watching, Ms. Frizzle?" Tim asked.

3

"Not just yet," the Friz answered. "First, I want you to meet someone."

I started to wriggle with excitement. This was what I had been waiting for.

"Phoebe," Ms. Frizzle said, "would you bring in our guest?"

I ran to the door, where my uncle Cecil Byrd was waiting. He's a little shy, like me. I grabbed hold of his arm and pulled him inside the room.

"Everyone," I said proudly, "this is my uncle Cecil."

Uncle Cecil stood in front of the class beside me. He had his bird-watching binoculars around his neck. With his long legs and pointy nose, I guess he looked a little like a stork.

"G'day, mates," Uncle Cecil said. "Call me Cecil." Uncle Cecil is from Australia and has a neat accent.

"G'day, Cecil," the kids said back with a few giggles.

"We're doing a project on birds," Ms. Frizzle explained.

"Righto," Uncle Cecil said. "Who can tell me what a bird is?"

Dorothy Ann jumped up before anyone else had a chance to let out a peep.

"According to my research," she began, "all birds share these characteristics. . . ."

From Dorothy Ann's Notebook

Birds of a Feather

Birds are animals that have feathers. They lay eggs in nests and keep the eggs warm until the young birds hatch.

Birds are warm-blooded and most birds fly – but not all.

"You're no birdbrain," Uncle Cecil told D.A. with a wink. "That was an excellent report."

"We're studying birds from all around the world," Ralphie said.

"Uncle Cecil is an ornithologist," I explained. "That's someone who studies birds."

"My favorite bird is the penguin," Uncle Cecil said. "I've been to Antarctica twice to study them. That's not to be confused with the *Arctic*. That's in the north, and *no* penguins are there!"

"Cool!" Carlos said.

"Cold, actually," Uncle Cecil corrected him. "Really, really cold!"

"How can birds survive in such a cold place?" Wanda asked.

"They wear snowsuits!" Arnold blurted out.

"It may look as if penguins wear suits," Uncle Cecil said. "But those are really feathers. A penguin's feathers can keep out freezing cold and winds that would turn humans into ice."

"We aren't going to Antarctica, are we, Ms. Frizzle?" Arnold asked nervously.

"No, Arnold, we're just going to a bird sanctuary," Ms. Frizzle said. "Since the weather is turning cold, a lot of birds are migrating. It's a great time to watch for birds."

From Cecil's Penguin Papers

Penguins are birds that don't fly. There are 17 species of penguins. Most live in the cooler waters of the southern hemisphere, including those of Antarctica. Others live near Australia, Africa, and South America.
Penguins don't have wings, but they do have flippers. They use their flippers for swimming. Some penguins spend 75% of their time in water. But all penguins breed on land or on sea ice that is attached to land.

Ms. Frizzle pulled out a pair of binoculars from a big box on her desk.

"Look, I have a pair of binoculars for each of you. They're great for nature watching."

We each took a pair of binoculars and hung them around our necks. Then we grabbed our coats and backpacks. Ms. Frizzle told us to bundle up. Then she grabbed Liz and headed for the bus.

I noticed that Uncle Cecil was still carrying his briefcase. He takes it everywhere with him. I checked out the sign on it. It read KEEP OUT!! THIS MEANS YOU!

"Uncle Cecil," I asked, "what is in there?"

"It's top secret, Phoebe," Cecil whispered. "Top secret!"

"You mean you can't tell even me?" I asked.

"Not now," Cecil said. "Maybe later."

We piled inside the Magic School Bus. Little did we know what would happen next!

CHAPTER 2

The Magic School Bus was chugging along the road. All of us kids had our binoculars out. We were staring at everything we passed — trees, birds, even people in cars!

I was sitting next to Uncle Cecil. We were right behind Ms. Frizzle, who was driving the bus. I noticed that Uncle Cecil was holding his briefcase very carefully in his lap.

"Uncle Cecil," I whispered, "can't you tell me what's —"

I was interrupted by a shout from Ralphie in back of us.

"Stop that, Dorothy Ann!"

Dorothy Ann was examining Ralphie through her binoculars.

"But Ralphie," she said, "you're such an interesting specimen."

"I am not a specimen," Ralphie protested. "I'm a *human*."

"Well, almost," D.A. said, rolling her eyes.

Just then, Ms. Frizzle asked Uncle Cecil a question. They began talking about migration patterns and other things that were way over my head.

I started to squirm in my seat. It was really getting hot in the bus. We were all bundled up in our winter coats.

"I'm hot!" Arnold complained. He was sitting in the first seat across the aisle.

"Me too," I said. "This bus feels like an oven."

"Ms. Frizzle," Arnold said, "can we turn on the air-conditioning?"

But Ms. Frizzle was too wrapped up in driving and talking to Uncle Cecil. She didn't hear a word Arnold said.

"Hey, Phoebe," Arnold said. "Can you reach the air-conditioning button on the dashboard?"

I looked at the dashboard of the Magic School Bus. There were lots of strange buttons. But one was red with a silver icicle on it.

"I don't think we should touch anything without asking Ms. Frizzle first," I told Arnold.

"Well, I'm toasting like a marshmallow," Arnold said. "I've got to do something!"

Arnold reached out his hand and pushed hard on the red button with the icicle. I saw Liz try to stop him with a flick of her tail.

Ms. Frizzle must have seen him out of the corner of her eye, because she shouted, "Arnold, no!"

But it was too late!

"What did I do?" Arnold yelled as the Magic School Bus started to shake and change shape.

"You hit the Big Chill button!" Ms. Frizzle answered. Her voice sounded strained. Her eyes were fixed on the dashboard as it changed into something with all kinds of dials and flashing lights. I knew I had seen that before. The Magic School Bus was turning into the Magic School Jet!

"What's happening? Where are we going?" I asked the Friz.

But my voice was drowned out by the roar of the engines. Then signs began to flash on the screens over our seats.

FASTEN SEAT BELTS!

PREPARE FOR TAKEOFF!

The roar of the engines got louder. Suddenly, we were pressed back into our seats by the force of the jet's acceleration. I looked out the window and saw the ground whizzing by!

The Magic School Jet was taxiing for takeoff. Uncle Cecil tightened his seat belt and checked mine. I noticed that he looked a little flustered. After all, this was his first field trip on the Magic School Bus!

"At least it's cooler in here," Arnold said.

"Don't worry, Arnold," Ms. Frizzle said. "You'll be plenty cool soon." I noticed that familiar twinkle in her eye. But that wasn't all I noticed.

"Arnold, look!" I said. "Her dress changed!"

We both stared at Ms. Frizzle's dress. It was still mostly blue. But most of the birds had disappeared from the sky. Now there were a bunch of birds on what looked like ice. When I looked closely, I could tell they were penguins.

"Ms. Frizzle," Arnold asked nervously, "where are we going?"

Just then, the jet took off. Soon, we were cruising high above the clouds. Ms. Frizzle flicked on the automatic pilot and then stood up to face the class.

"Thanks to Arnold," she said, "we've just changed our plans for this field trip. Once you press the Big Chill button, there's no turning back. We're on an express flight to Antarctica — the Big Chill at the bottom of the world!"

"Antarctica!" at least ten voices said at once.

From the Desk of Ms. Frizzle

The Ends of the World

Some people confuse Antarctica with the Arctic.

Antarctica is a vast area of frozen land that surrounds the South Pole. The Arctic is a huge frozen ocean that surrounds the North Pole.

Antarctica is:
- the world's coldest continent.
- the world's windiest continent.
- the world's highest continent.
- the world's least populated continent.

"I think it's time for a geography lesson," the Friz announced. She popped open an overhead compartment and pulled out a big world globe. Liz jumped onto the globe and pointed to Antarctica with her tail.

"We're heading south," Ms. Frizzle said. "All the way south!"

"Hey, look out the window," Carlos yelled. "I think we're over a rain forest now."

We all leaned over to the windows to see. Below us was a velvety green carpet of trees. It seemed to go on forever!

Ms. Frizzle pointed to Brazil on the globe. "We must be right about here — just above the Amazon rain forest."

Dorothy Ann was busy with her calculator. "According to my calculations," she announced, "we have gone over the equator."

"You're right, Dorothy Ann," Ms. Frizzle said. "Now we're in the southern hemisphere. And it's not winter here — it's summer!"

"If it's summer in Antarctica," I asked my uncle, "does that mean the whole place will melt?"

"Jolly good question, Phoebe," Uncle Cecil said. "But the answer is no. Even in the summer, Antarctica is freezing. In fact, if Antarctica melted, there would be so much water that the whole world would be flooded!"

"How many minutes until we get to Antarctica?" Ralphie asked. "I want to see some penguins."

"It won't be long," Ms. Frizzle answered. "Meanwhile, let's get ready."

She pressed a button on the jet's control panel. A second later, the compartments over our seats popped open. Orange packages fell into each of our laps.

"Start putting on your expedition gear," the Friz ordered. "It may be summer in Antarctica, but you still need to bundle up! They don't call it the Big Chill for nothing!"

CHAPTER 3

We spent the rest of the flight putting on our cold-weather gear. Thermal underwear went on first. Then came several more layers of clothes.

"No wonder penguins walk so funny," Arnold said as he waddled down the aisle. "All this padding makes it hard to move!"

"Arnold, waddle back to your seat," Ms. Frizzle ordered. "We're ready for touchdown."

I looked up at the flashing sign over my seat.

FASTEN SEAT BELTS!

PREPARE FOR LANDING!

"Where will we land, Uncle Cecil? I don't see an airport anywhere!" I asked as I checked my seat belt.

"Planes and boats both come to Antarctica," Uncle Cecil said. "There are scientists who live on Antarctica, especially during the summer. Several countries have research stations here. Even tourists come to visit!"

The plane was dropping lower and lower and closer and closer to the water. Suddenly, we could see the ice-blue ocean below us. There were big chunks of ice floating on it.

"Ms. Frizzle, I don't see an airport," Ralphie cried out. "Are we going to crash-land in the water?"

Ms. Frizzle was too busy to answer Ralphie. I saw her punching buttons and checking readouts.

Beside me, Uncle Cecil was clutching his briefcase to his chest.

"Phoebe," he said nervously, "are you sure Ms. Frizzle knows what she's doing?"

Just when it looked as if we were going to nose-dive into the water, something amazing happened.

The Magic School Jet turned into a Magic School Boat! Ms. Frizzle wasn't at the controls of a plane anymore. She now had her hands on a big boat wheel. And all of us kids were sitting on a bench inside the cabin of a boat, instead of in our plane seats.

"First Mate Byrd, I need your help," Ms. Frizzle called out to Uncle Cecil.

"Aye-aye, Captain," Uncle Cecil said. He jumped up to join Ms. Frizzle at the wheel. Together, they studied a map of Antarctica.

"Ahoy, mates," Carlos shouted. "Check out the whale!"

We all ran to where Carlos was standing, staring out the window. It didn't take long to see the whale. It was blowing a big spout of water into the air. The force of exhaled air was so strong, it pushed up the surface water into a big spray.

We thought the spout was cool, but then, a huge blue whale broke out of the water right in front of us. It was over eighty feet long. I could see why it's the largest mammal on Earth!

"That whale doesn't eat boats, does it?" Arnold asked in a shaky voice.

"Not to worry," Uncle Cecil said with a chuckle. "Blue whales eat little sea animals called krill."

"Do I look like a krill?" Arnold asked, ducking so the blue whale couldn't see him.

"This is how krill looks, Arnold," the Friz said, flipping open a book. "No family resemblance to you!"

From the Desk of Ms. Frizzle

Little Krill in the Big Chill

Krill are little shrimplike sea creatures. Antarctic krill are only about $1\frac{1}{2}$ inches long. Swarms of krill can be several miles wide. That many krill can make the ocean look pink!

Whales, seals, penguins, and fish eat krill. Fishing boats catch krill, too.

"I want to see some penguins," Ralphie complained. He waddled around on the deck flapping his arms like penguin flippers.

"It won't be long," Uncle Cecil told him. "Penguins eat krill, too. There are probably some in the water around us right now."

Everyone whipped out their binoculars to look. Suddenly, Dorothy Ann let out a shriek.

"Look at the island ahead of us," she said. "There are funny black-and-white birds all over it!"

"Penguin sighting!" Uncle Cecil yelled. He sounded as excited as I felt.

We all ran to the front of the boat and trained our binoculars on the island. I couldn't believe my eyes. They were the cutest animals I had ever seen.

"Let's get closer," Uncle Cecil said to Ms. Frizzle. "It's a whole colony of chinstraps."

"Are they really wearing chin straps?" I asked Uncle Cecil.

"No, that's just a pattern in their feathers," Uncle Cecil explained. "There are more chinstraps in Antarctic waters than any other kind of penguin."

**From Cecil's Penguin Papers
Chinstraps**

There are almost twelve million chinstrap penguins in Antarctica! Why are they called chinstraps? They have a narrow band of black feathers that goes under their "chin" from ear to ear.

These little penguins are only 28 to 29 inches tall. Chinstraps may be small, but they are the boldest penguins of all.

There were so many chinstraps on the island you could hardly see the rocks!

As we got closer to the island, I noticed a smell. The smell got stronger and stronger. Everyone else had started to hold their noses shut, too.

"EWWW, what's that?" Wanda asked.

Cecil laughed and pointed to the penguins. "That's penguin guano you smell. The island is covered with it."

"Gross!" Wanda said. "They need some air freshener."

I noticed that Liz had turned yellow-green and had her tongue sticking out.

"Full speed ahead, Ms. Frizzle," Uncle Cecil said. "Let's get out into some fresh air and find some other penguins."

I waved good-bye to the chinstraps with my free hand. The other one was still holding my nose shut. I couldn't believe they could stand that smell. I was happy when we were back in the fresh, freezing air.

"Ms. Frizzle, Ms. Frizzle," Ralphie called out. "Is that Antarctica up ahead of us?"

We all turned to look where Ralphie was pointing. Ahead of us was a huge chunk of ice!

"That's just an iceberg, Ralphie," the Friz said.

"Just an iceberg?" Wanda exclaimed. "It's so huge!"

She was right. The iceberg rose straight up out of the water and had lots of white peaks. "And that's only the tip of the iceberg!" Tim said.

Very Big Ice Cubes!
by Tim

Only the tip of an iceberg is above the water. Ninety percent of an iceberg is hidden below the surface. A lot of icebergs are big. But some are gigantic! In 1987, an iceberg named B-9 was sighted. It was 96 miles long and 22 miles wide. That's about the size of the state of Delaware!

I started to get nervous. I remembered that the *Titanic* sunk after hitting an iceberg. "Ms. Frizzle, are you sure our boat is safe this close to the iceberg?" I asked.

"Not to worry, Phoebe," the Friz answered. "The *Frozen Frizzle* will keep us ship-shape."

My heart was beating fast the whole time we passed by the iceberg. It made our boat look like a toy floating in the ocean.

"There it is!" Uncle Cecil suddenly shouted. "Antarctica!" He pointed to some huge white cliffs in the distance. It looked like an iceberg, but even bigger.

Ms. Frizzle steered the boat toward the coastline. Suddenly, there was a loud bang on the side of the *Frozen Frizzle*. We felt the whole ship shake.

"Uncle Cecil," I whispered in a nervous voice, "what was that?"

"Keep your cool, Phoebe," Cecil said. "We just hit a piece of pack ice. It's just an ice cube compared to that iceberg we passed before."

Antarctica was getting a little scary, but Ms. Frizzle stayed on course. Suddenly, we sighted a huge cliff of ice ahead of us!

"What is that?" Carlos asked.

"You're looking at the Ross Ice Shelf," Uncle Cecil explained.

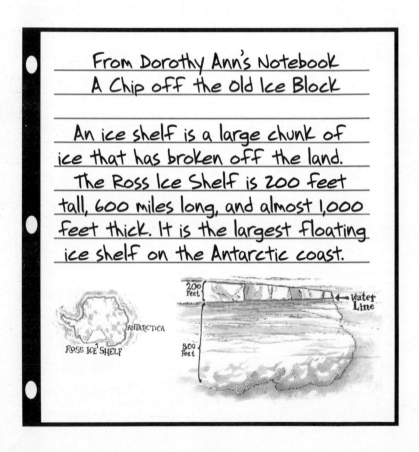

From Dorothy Ann's Notebook
A Chip off the Old Ice Block

An ice shelf is a large chunk of ice that has broken off the land.

The Ross Ice Shelf is 200 feet tall, 600 miles long, and almost 1,000 feet thick. It is the largest floating ice shelf on the Antarctic coast.

I noticed that Dorothy Ann was busy flipping through her notebook. I knew it was only a matter of time. . . .

"According to my research," Dorothy Ann announced, "an ice shelf is formed at the edge of Antarctica."

"See the mountain behind the Ross Ice Shelf?" Uncle Cecil asked. "It's called Terror Mountain."

"It's two miles high and made up of tons of ice," the Friz said.

"I think I know why it's called Terror Mountain," Wanda said, shaking in her boots as she looked straight up at the jagged ice.

By the time we passed the Ross Ice Shelf, we were all shivering. Ms. Frizzle went belowdecks and came up with a big pile of yellow parkas.

"Bundle up!" she ordered. "This is no time to get cold feet!"

CHAPTER 2

Even though we had on our heavy coats, we all felt really underdressed when we saw the next penguins.

Arnold was the first to spot one.

"Penguin, ho!" he yelled.

Arnold pointed to a black-and-white penguin standing at the end of a cliff. As we rounded the cliff, we saw a whole colony of penguins!

"Look, they're all wearing tuxedos!" Wanda yelled.

"They're dressed up for a penguin party!" Keesha added.

The penguins were waddling around the

cliff. They looked all dressed up with nowhere to go!

Uncle Cecil came over with an excited look on his face. "Those are Adélie penguins," he said, "and they aren't wearing suits. They're just wearing their feathers — very special feathers."

I noticed that Uncle Cecil was nervously patting his briefcase the whole time he was talking about the penguins. Something mysterious was in there!

Ms. Frizzle checked the clock in the cabin of the *Frozen Frizzle*. "It's time to set up camp for the day," she said. "Let's go ashore."

I began to wonder how we were going to do that. But never fear — when you have the Magic School Bus near!

As we got closer to the shore, the Magic School Boat turned into a Magic School Snowmobile. Soon, we were chugging along the ice on our big runners. The snowmobile wasn't as roomy as the boat — but it was exciting! We drove right through where the penguins were swarming around. Tim drew a lot of great sketches. It was like being on a snow safari!

A little farther inland, Ms. Frizzle brought the snowmobile to a stop.

"Pile out," she ordered. "We'll set up our base camp here. The Magic School Bus needs to recharge its batteries and we need to keep warm."

One by one, we jumped out of the snowmobile. The air around us was superclear. And the snow was superwhite. It was so white and bright it hurt our eyes.

"I need some shades!" Carlos yelled.

"Me too," everyone else chimed in. We had to squint to see!

The snowmobile was equipped with everything we needed. Ms. Frizzle and Uncle Cecil passed out special sunglasses for all of us to wear. Then Dorothy Ann took some pictures of us posing in our Antarctic gear.

From the Desk of Ms. Frizzle

Travel Warning!

The Antarctic skies are clear and clean. There is no dust, no pollution, and little moisture in the air. With the glare from the sun and reflection from snow and ice, it's a very white, bright place. For human eyes, that hurts! Without sunglasses, people can get snow blindness.

We were having a great time.

"Class," Ms. Frizzle called out, "it's later than you think. Who wants to have a sleepover tonight?"

We all got excited about a sleepover. Ms. Frizzle said we could look for more penguins tomorrow. Then she asked for help with setting up our tent for the night.

I ran over to help right away. One thing was for sure — I wanted a warm, cozy place to sleep!

Setting up, our tent looked like a big dome.

"Ms. Frizzle," Tim asked, "will we be sleeping on land or ice tonight?"

"Good question, Tim," the Friz answered. "There's land under your feet — but it's a long way down. Tonight, you'll be sleeping on an ice cap!"

Making our camp was hard work. We were all tired out. Arnold let out a big yawn. Then Wanda yawned. Soon, we had all caught a case of the yawns.

From the Desk of Ms. Frizzle

Antarctica's Ice Cap

Antarctica is a large landmass. But almost the entire continent is covered by an ice cap. Even in the summer, most of the ice cap is about a mile thick! In fact, the ice on top of Antarctica weighs so much that it pushes the land under it below sea level.

The ice cap is always growing. It has been growing over millions of years! Each year, only a few inches of snow fall. But the snow rarely ever melts.

"When is it going to get dark?" Carlos asked, rubbing his eyes. "I think it's past my bedtime."

Dorothy Ann whipped out her handy notebook.

"Hold on just a minute, Carlos," she said. "I've got the answer right here."

D.A. leafed through her book. Then she looked at Carlos and said, "Never."

"Never what?" Carlos asked.

"It will never get dark tonight," Dorothy Ann said. "The sun never completely sets on Antarctica in the summer."

"This place is way weird," Carlos said. "I may have to go to sleep with my sunglasses on."

From Dorothy Ann's Notebook
The Sun Never Sets

For several weeks each summer, it's light around the clock in Antarctica. Earth tilts at a steep angle toward the sun. So the sun never sets on the South Pole. In the winter, when the Antarctic tilts away from the sun, there is total darkness.

We all crowded inside the tent and laid out our sleeping bags on the floor. I felt something small and cold crawl in with me. It was Liz, looking homesick. I fell asleep thinking about how much fun it would be to play with the penguins the next day.

You've never been on Antarctica before!

I've never been so cold!

CHAPTER 5

A really strange sound woke me up the next morning. I opened my eyes and couldn't figure out where I was. Then it hit me — I was in Antarctica!

I saw Uncle Cecil cooking some oatmeal for breakfast over the camp stove. I heard the strange sound again and got up fast.

"Uncle Cecil," I whispered. "What is that noise?"

"Not to worry, Phoebe," he said. "It's just a male penguin, looking for his mate."

Before the penguin found his mate, he woke up the whole class. Yawning and grumbling, we all sat down to eat breakfast.

Ms. Frizzle was sitting on the tent floor typing on her laptop.

"What's up for today, Ms. Frizzle?" Tim asked.

"I want to study the weather more," she said. "And you can go find more penguins."

We all bundled up and stepped outside. Whew! What a wake-up call that was!

"What makes the winds so cold?" D.A. asked with chattering teeth.

"Those are katabatic winds," Ms. Frizzle explained.

"What are katabatic winds?" I asked. "They sure sound scary."

From the Desk of Ms. Frizzle

Those Crazy Katabatic Winds

Antarctica has the strongest and coldest winds in the world. Katabatic winds are formed when cold, dense air flows down from the ice cap to the coast.

"Can we go play with the penguins now?" Ralphie asked.

"I'm going to stay here to take measurements. But you go on," Ms. Frizzle said. "Be sure to take notes for your reports. And try to find Cecil. He seems to have wandered off somewhere."

We walked over to a group of Adélie penguins that were sheltered from the winds by a hill of ice.

"They aren't at all afraid of us," Keesha said.

"This book says that adult Adélie penguins have no natural predators on land," D.A. shared, "so they have no instincts to be afraid on land."

We stood and watched the penguins.

"I think they're using sign language," Wanda said.

The penguins were nodding at one another. It looked like they were motioning with their flippers. Then we heard the braying sound that had woken us all up this morning.

"That's a male, looking for his mate," I said, feeling important to know so much.

"Let's follow him," Carlos said.

Carefully, we trailed behind the male penguin who was waddling across the ice. He led us to a female who was sitting on a pile of rocks. The female got up and let the male take her place. We spied two penguin eggs in between the rocks.

"They are going to have babies!" Wanda gushed.

Dorothy Ann started flipping through her field guide again. "Listen to this!" she said.

From Dorothy Ann's Notebook
Adélies and More Adélies

Adélie penguins have their young during the warm weeks of summer. A male and female penguin build a rocky nest on high ground. The eggs are laid in early November. The eggs need to be kept warm all the time. The male and female take turns keeping the eggs warm and protecting the eggs from being eaten. If everything goes right, penguin chicks hatch after about thirty days.

"I hope we get to see a chick hatch," Wanda said. "Penguin babies must be so cute!"

"I wish Uncle Cecil was here," I said. "He'd know when the eggs will hatch."

"Look over there," Arnold said. "Isn't that Cecil's hat?"

Arnold was right. I could see the top of Uncle Cecil's funny thermal hat sticking up above a pile of rocks not far away.

"Let's go ask him about the eggs," Wanda said.

We all ran over to find Uncle Cecil, but when we came around the rocks he had a shocked look on his face. Then I noticed his top secret briefcase was wide open.

"Uncle Cecil," I gasped. "What are you doing?"

We all stared down at the things Uncle Cecil had spread out in his briefcase. There were two plastic squeeze bottles filled with some kind of liquid. There were some penguin feathers. And there was a laptop computer with a scientific formula on the screen.

"I . . . I . . . I guess I can't keep it a secret anymore," Uncle Cecil stammered.

"Is this your experiment on penguins?" I asked.

"Yes," Uncle Cecil said, "but it's not done yet. Do you all promise not to tell anyone about this until I publish my findings?"

"Promise!" we all said together.

Uncle Cecil picked up one of the plastic bottles. "This bottle contains a secret formula that I developed. I began by studying penguin feathers that I found on the ground."

"What's so special about penguin feathers?" Arnold asked.

"The feathers have a special oil on them. That's what keeps the birds warm and dry — even in the Antarctic," Cecil explained.

"And like a lot of scientists, you want to find out how to use the oil to help humans, right?" Dorothy Ann asked with excitement.

"Exactly!" Uncle Cecil answered. "Just think . . . it could help millions of people."

"What's the next step in your research?" Carlos asked.

"I want to test the secret formula on myself," Uncle Cecil answered. "And that's what I'm going to do — right now!"

We held our breath while Uncle Cecil took off his parka and held the plastic bottle over his body. But just as he was ready to squirt it over himself, a penguin jumped up on the rocks behind him and made a loud squawking sound.

The rest happened fast! Uncle Cecil whirled around in surprise. Then he slipped on the ice. As he fell, he accidentally squeezed the bottle. Out squirted the secret formula — all over us!

Before we could say, "secret formula," the eight of us turned into Adélie penguins! Uncle Cecil stared at us in shock. But he wasn't as shocked as we were! I looked down at my short feathery body and my small webbed feet. I didn't know what to do!

But then I saw Arnold, Wanda, and the rest of the kid-penguins waddling toward the ocean. I waddled fast to catch up with them.

Suddenly, I had the urge to jump into icy-cold water!

CHAPTER 6

I waddled after Dorothy Ann as fast as I could. I knew I had to hurry so I wouldn't lose the rest of the class. My new penguin legs were so short I could take only baby steps!

From the back, I couldn't tell the real penguins from the kid-penguins. How would Ms. Frizzle ever find us?

That made me remember Uncle Cecil. I turned around and looked back. He was just getting up off the ice. He looked really confused. I saw him looking at our group of penguins. Did he even know what had happened to us?

"Uncle Cecil!" I tried to call out. But as

soon as my voice got loud enough, it turned into a penguin bray. I tried to wave a flipper at him. But instead I caught the attention of a bunch of real penguins around me. They waved back to me with their flippers.

Suddenly, the urge to go for a cold swim was too much to resist. I took one last glance back at Uncle Cecil. Then I ran for the water after the rest of the kid-penguins.

Ahead of me, Dorothy Ann turned around and gave me a nod. I heard her voice say, "Watch me!"

Then D.A. did something really cool! She flopped down on the ice on her stomach and went whizzing down the icy slope like a sled. I could see Arnold, Tim, and Carlos push off on their stomachs, too. They used their little feet to get themselves going.

I wasn't going to miss out on the fun! I flopped down on the ice, feeling a little scared at first. But then instinct took over! My feet pushed me off — and I was streaking down that slope just behind Carlos.

Wheeeee! I was surfing over that ice like a pro! Then, something ahead caught my attention. The end of the ice shelf! *Where are the brakes?* I asked myself. I was afraid that if I dove into the water I'd freeze, but I couldn't stop myself!

I tried to slow down. Flippers didn't work. Feet didn't work. There was no stopping now. I flew off the end of the cliff.

SPLASH! I held my breath as I torpedoed into the water. I couldn't believe it, but the water felt great! Uncle Cecil was right about penguin feathers. They do keep you nice and warm. I twisted and turned my body around, feeling right at home.

SPLASH! Another penguin rocketed into the water beside me. I caught a glimpse of the penguin's face. It was Arnold — looking really surprised. The two of us swam through the water beside each other. Together, we tried out our new swimming equipment.

Our flippers made great propellers. One flip and we'd go shooting through the water. We started out slow. Soon we were clocking about five miles per hour. But we weren't as fast yet as Carlos and Dorothy Ann. They went zooming by at about seven miles per hour.

Even more fun was avoiding the ice chunks around us. Our feet and tails came in handy for that. One flick of our tails and we'd curve around a major piece of pack ice.

Arnold and I practiced our swimming techniques for a while. Then I felt my penguin tummy sort of growl. I was hungry! And I

didn't want freeze-dried chicken. I was in the mood for some fresh seafood.

Yum! I saw a tender little squid on a rock below me. I scooped it up with my bill and swallowed it whole. It was a good start, but now on to the main course.

I shot through the water, looking for krill. Ahead, I noticed that the water was a pinkish color. Just the sight of it made my stomach growl. I torpedoed into the colony of krill, my mouth wide open. I munched on a mouthful of krill and then went back for more.

We played around in the water for a while, then we met up with the rest of the kids. Dorothy Ann waved her flipper and nodded a couple of times. Even as a penguin, Dorothy Ann could be bossy.

Dorothy Ann took the lead and started to swim fast through the water. Then she did something really amazing. She leaped right out of the water into the air — just like a porpoise. We all followed right behind her. Porpoising was great. It felt kind of like flying!

Why Penguins Porpoise
by Phoebe Penguin

Penguins are really good swimmers. Some species can go up to 15 miles per hour. But they can go even faster by leaping out of the water like a porpoise. There's less resistance going through the air than the water. So this increases their speed.

Porpoising lets the penguins grab some quick breaths of air. It also makes it harder for predators to catch them.

What Makes Penguins Porpoise Such Good Swimmers?

Flippers!

Webbed Feet!

I'd been having so much fun that I forgot about the Antarctic food chain. We penguins eat krill and squid. But lots of other things eat us. Leopard seals, killer whales — just to name a couple!

Suddenly, I felt a sense of danger. My instincts told me to get back to land where I would be safe — fast!

A few feet from the ice, my body did an amazing thing. Using my flippers and feet, I made a huge jump out of the water. I felt myself leaping through the air toward the icy cliff. Just at the last second, I cleared the top of the cliff. Touchdown! I breathed a sigh of relief and smoothed down my feathers. Whew!

I stood by the edge of the cliff, looking out to sea. I caught a glimpse of a bunch of penguins porpoising in the water. I could tell it was the other kids, still playing in the water. Then I saw something else that made my penguin heart start to pound!

A leopard seal was cutting through the water. Right toward Dorothy Ann!

CHAPTER 7

I couldn't waste another second. The leopard seal was going in for the kill. I had to warn the others!

"Dorothy Ann! Tim! Carlos!" I started to scream their names one by one. The words came out of my bill like a loud braying sound. I was talking and braying at the same time! I hopped up and down on the icy cliff and kept braying.

Finally, D.A. saw me. Right away, she knew something was wrong. She took off for the cliff, waving her flipper at the others. The other kid-penguins shot through the water after her.

With their black backs turned to the sea, the penguins were hard to see in the water. The seal lost sight of them. It stopped swimming and searched the water. By the time it had found D.A. again, she was leaping from the water up onto the ice shelf.

Dorothy Ann gave a bray of relief. Arnold, Keesha, Carlos, Tim, Wanda, and Ralphie all hopped up onto the cliff. Everyone was happy to get back onto safe ground.

"Wow, that was close!" Dorothy Ann said.

"It's a cold, cruel world out there," Tim added.

We hung out on the cliff for a while. There were hundreds of Adélie penguins around us. They gave us some strange looks, but otherwise ignored us.

"You know what I think is weird?" Carlos said.

"What?" Wanda asked.

"What's really weird is the smell," Carlos said.

"What smell?" Wanda asked.

"That's what I mean!" Carlos said. "I don't even smell the guano anymore."

"Maybe . . . maybe we're not human anymore!" Wanda said with a sniffle.

"What if we never get back to the Magic School Bus?" Arnold asked.

I tried to think of something hopeful to say.

"Ms. Frizzle will save us . . . and Uncle Cecil," I told Arnold. "You just wait and see."

"Meanwhile," Dorothy Ann said, "let's check out some penguin nests. I still want to see a chick hatch!"

As usual, Dorothy Ann's mind was on science!

We waddled over to where dozens of penguins were baby-sitting their eggs. Two of the penguins seemed to be having a fight.

"Look, one is stealing a rock from the other one," Wanda said.

"Penguins do that," Dorothy Ann explained. "I read that we have to compete for the best nesting sites."

"What do you mean *we*?" Wanda asked.

"Oh, right, I mean *they*," Dorothy Ann corrected herself.

Just then, a female Adélie penguin got off her nest. She waddled up to Arnold. She barked some orders at him in penguin language.

Arnold just stared at her. Then she took her flippers and pushed him toward the nest.

"No, no," Arnold protested. "You've got the wrong guy. I'm not your mate."

The female penguin didn't pay any attention to Arnold's noises. She made him sit on top of her egg. Then she waddled away toward the water. She threw back a warning glance at Arnold not to move!

"Looks like you can't get up until your wife gets back, Arnold," Tim said.

"You'd better keep those eggs nice and toasty," Carlos said. Then he laughed until he brayed.

"You'd better not leave me!" Arnold begged. "Please!"

It looked as if we were stuck baby-sitting a penguin egg. But when would the mother come back?

Meanwhile, back at the camp, Ms. Frizzle was measuring the ice caps and taking notes.

She saw Uncle Cecil come slipping and sliding across the ice. The look on his face spelled trouble!

"Cecil," the Friz gasped, "what's the matter?"

"My experiment backfired," Uncle Cecil moaned. "I turned the kids into penguins!"

"How did you do that?" Ms. Frizzle asked with a worried look on her face.

"I squirted them with my top secret formula," Uncle Cecil explained. "It was all an accident . . . but now they're penguins. And I can't find them anywhere!"

Ms. Frizzle thought for a moment. "We've got a penguin puzzle that we have to solve!" Then she added, "Maybe it takes one to know one."

"You mean . . . you mean, I should turn into a penguin?" Uncle Cecil stammered.

"Do you have enough secret formula left?" the Friz asked.

"A whole bottle," Uncle Cecil answered.

"Hand it over," Ms. Frizzle ordered. "And get ready to waddle!"

Uncle Cecil took the last bottle of formula out of his briefcase. He handed it to Ms. Frizzle and shut his eyes.

Seconds later, a large emperor penguin stood in front of the Friz. Liz took one look and jumped inside the Friz's parka pocket.

"Is that you, Cecil?" Ms. Frizzle asked in amazement.

From Cecil's Penguin Papers
The Emperor of Penguins

The emperor penguin is the biggest penguin of all. It grows up to 3.7 feet tall and can weigh more than 60 pounds. That's about half the size of a human adult.

Emperor penguins are the only penguins that breed during the cold, dark winter in Antarctica. After the female lays a single egg, she goes off to sea. The male stays on land with the egg. He keeps it warm on his feet under a "brood pouch" for 72 days!

The emperor males huddle together with their eggs for warmth and protection. They take turns being on the warm inside and the cold outside of their huddle. These dedicated dads live off stored fat during this time and lose about half of their body weight!

"I think so," Uncle Cecil's voice said. Then it turned into a penguin bray.

"Good luck," the Friz called as Uncle Cecil waddled off.

Uncle Cecil headed toward a crowd of Adélie penguins.

"Phoebe," he called out. "Arnold, Dorothy Ann, Carlos!"

None of the penguins answered to the names. Uncle Cecil walked from one group of penguins to another. He had to fight off the urge to take a dip in the ocean. He knew he had to keep his penguin mind on the kids!

Just then, he walked by an Adélie penguin nest. A little Adélie chick was being fed by its parents. Uncle Cecil took mental notes to add to his research.

From Cecil's Penguin Papers
Adélie Baby Food

Adélie parents take turns keeping their chicks warm and fed. While one watches the nest, the other goes into the ocean to catch krill. The penguins carry the krill back to the nest in their stomachs. Then they regurgitate it to feed their chicks.

Uncle Cecil wandered through the Adélie colony for an hour. Then he had to give up. There were thousands of Adélie penguins. And none of them answered to his call.

Slowly, he waddled back to camp. He hated to tell Ms. Frizzle the news. They might not see Phoebe and the others again. Ever!

CHAPTER 8

Back at camp, Ms. Frizzle saw a big emperor penguin waddle toward the tent. Alone.

"Cecil, where are they?" she called out.

"I couldn't find them," Uncle Cecil answered. "There are Adélie penguins everywhere!"

"I'm not giving up!" the Friz exclaimed. She ran over to the Magic School Snowmobile, climbed inside, and started the engine.

There was a loud roar. The Magic School Bus was at it again! A big propeller popped out of the top. The treads turned into skis. And the snowmobile turned into a snow helicopter.

Ms. Frizzle sat in the cockpit. She

motioned to Uncle Cecil. "We're going on a search mission."

Uncle Cecil waddled over to the copter's door and hopped inside.

Then, with a roar of the engine, the copter took off. It flew straight up into the clear Antarctic air.

Ms. Frizzle flew out above the ice shelf.

"Where did you last see the kids, Cecil?" Ms. Frizzle asked.

"I was right behind a pile of rocks," Uncle Cecil said. "It was right down there. A bit behind us."

The Friz made a loop in the sky. Then she zoomed down to the rocks and hovered for a minute.

"Do you see them anywhere?" she asked. Uncle Cecil was sticking his penguin head out the window. He shook it sadly.

"Let's see, where else would I go if I were a penguin?" Ms. Frizzle asked herself.

She sighted the end of the ice shelf hanging over the water. She gained altitude and then flew over toward the water.

"There are hundreds and hundreds of penguins down there!" Uncle Cecil said with dismay.

"Not to worry, Cecil," the Friz exclaimed. "We'll find them!"

She dropped the bus-copter lower in the sky. The penguins on the ice below became excited by the noise. They milled around, look-ing up.

Suddenly, the Friz let out a gasp.

"Look, Cecil! Down to the right!"

Eight Adélie penguins were staring up at the bus-copter. And they had human faces!

"We found them!" Uncle Cecil yelled.

The eight of us kid-penguins were staring up at the sky with big smiles on our faces.

"They found us!" I yelled.

We watched Ms. Frizzle bring the bus-copter down onto the ice. All the other penguins ran away in every direction. But we were hopping up and down with joy.

"Ms. Frizzle!" Dorothy Ann yelled with relief.

"Uncle Cecil," I called out. "Is that you?"

Uncle Cecil ran up to me and gave me a big penguin hug.

"Come on," the Friz said. "Hop into the bus-copter. I'll fly you back to camp."

"But I can't leave," Arnold said. "I'm stuck on these eggs until my mate comes back."

"Arnold!" Ms. Frizzle said.

"I'm not really her mate," Arnold said. "But I can't leave the eggs until they hatch. The chicks could die."

Just then, there was a pecking noise. Arnold looked down at one of the eggs. A little bill was sticking out of the egg. A minute later,

more of the shell cracked open. A little flipper stuck out.

"Ohh, it's hatching!" I said. "Move over a little, Arnold!"

Arnold moved aside so we could all watch the baby penguin hatch. Soon it was free of its shell. Just then, its mother waddled up to the nest. She pushed Arnold aside and took over her baby.

From Cecil's Penguin Papers
Chilly Chicks

Most Adélie penguins incubate two eggs at a time. The little chicks hatch out at more or less the same time. One is usually stronger than the other and has a better chance of surviving.

When first born, the chicks are kept warm by their parents. But after two or three weeks, they develop a thick, woolly gray down. Then they join other chicks in creches, or nursery groups.

"I think it's time to leave, Arnold," Ms. Frizzle said with a twinkle in her eye. "But congratulations!"

Ms. Frizzle climbed into the bus-copter, and we all followed. It was very crowded inside with nine penguins! The bus-copter zoomed up into the sky.

"Whew! I'm getting hot in here," Arnold said.

"These feathers are great for icy weather," Uncle Cecil added. "But they are too much for inside."

"And we can't even take our coats off," Tim complained.

By the time the bus-copter landed back at camp, we penguins were steaming. We couldn't wait to get back into the ice-cold air!

After everyone piled out of the bus-copter, Uncle Cecil pulled on my flipper. "Phoebe, look," he said, pointing to the bus-copter floor.

A layer of penguin feathers was scattered on the floor. We had been shedding in the heat!

"I've got an idea," Uncle Cecil said. "Let's all go inside the tent."

"But it's hot in there," Arnold complained.

"Exactly!" Uncle Cecil said.

We went inside the tent, and I started sweating even more in my penguin suit!

"Will we be penguins forever?" Wanda asked Ms. Frizzle.

As soon as Arnold heard that, he started to cry. "I don't want to live in a zoo," he sobbed.

"I'm sure our parents would come to visit us," Tim said.

"I just want to be my old self," Arnold said.

"I think you're in luck, Arnold," Uncle Cecil said. "Take a look at the floor!"

All of us kid-penguins looked down at our feet. There were heaps of feathers and drops of oil all around us. The best news was that we had real feet! We were turning back into humans again.

"Yippee!" Carlos said. "I don't want to wear that suit anymore!"

I ran up and hugged Uncle Cecil. He was back to his old self, too.

"The heat must have reversed the effects of my formula," he said. "Thank goodness!"

"What will you do with your secret formula now, Cecil?" Dorothy Ann asked.

"It's all gone. And I'm not going to make any more," Uncle Cecil answered. "I've learned my lesson. Don't mess with Mother Nature!"

"But what about your work with penguins?" I asked.

"I'll keep studying them. I want to do as much as I can to protect them in the wild," Uncle Cecil said. "They are a fascinating bird."

"Start packing your things, class," Ms. Frizzle announced. "We're going home."

Everyone cheered, especially the eight of us who had been penguins. We had been worried there for a while. Antarctica is a nice place to visit. But I wouldn't want to live there!

Ms. Frizzle led us outside. The Magic School Bus had transformed into the Magic School Jet again. We pulled down the tent and packed everything up. We made sure we left Antarctica just as clean as we found it.

Then we got inside the jet and took off. As we flew over the ice shelf, we waved good-bye to the Adélie penguins. It looked like they were waving their flippers back at us. This was one adventure we would *never* forget!

CHAPTER 9

"Arnold, could you move your poster over?" Dorothy Ann asked. "It's crowding mine."

We were back in our classroom. And everything was back to normal!

Ms. Frizzle had decided we should do reports on Antarctica before going back to our bird projects. So the whole room was filled with pictures and posters about our trip.

But the main attraction was just coming in. Dorothy Ann, Arnold, Keesha, Carlos, Wanda, Ralphie, Tim, and I had all worked on it. It would be a surprise for Ms. Frizzle.

"Stand back, stand back," Carlos or-

dered as they brought it into the room. "We're coming through."

Tim, Carlos, and Wanda carried a big tray into the room. Something about two feet tall was standing on it, covered by a cloth. They set the tray down on a table.

"Phoebe," Carlos called out. "Are you ready?"

I nodded and walked over to pick up the edge of the cloth. Then I whisked it off.

Underneath was a life-size Adélie penguin — carved from ice!

"Cool!" Keesha said.

"Not cool," Carlos said with a laugh. "Cold. Really, really cold!"

Carlos was right. I knew we had taken the coolest field trip ever.

PENGUINS AND MORE PENGUINS

There are seventeen species of penguins in all. Four of these species live in Antarctica. But many other species live all over the world.

Rockhopper Penguins
by Carlos

Rockhopper Penguins have a bright crest on top of their heads. They breed in warmer, sub-Antarctic regions, away from pack ice.

Size: Rockhoppers weigh 6 pounds and stand 21 inches tall.

Fun Fact: Rockhoppers live on rocky islands where they jump from stone to stone – which is how they got their name!

Rockhopper Penguin

Galápagos Penguins
by Keesha

Galápagos penguins live on the Galápagos Islands. Because these islands are located at the equator, the waters are warm – not all penguins live in cold climates! Galápagos penguins have two bands of brown feathers on their faces and their bills are slender.

Size: They weigh 5 pounds and are $1\frac{1}{2}$ feet tall.

Fun Fact: Gálapagos penguins do not migrate.

Galapagos Penguin

African Penguins
by Ralphie

Did you ever think a penguin could live in Africa? Well, they do. African penguins live on islands off the south-western coast of Africa. They are also called black-footed penguins. Unfortunately, they are now endangered.

Size: They are 7 pounds and 18 inches tall.

Fun Fact: These penguins are somewhat mysterious. They are the least studied species.

Macaroni Penguins

by D. A.

   Macaroni penguins live on islands on the edge of Antarctica, as well as on islands that lie south of Africa and the Americas. They make their nests on cliffs and hillsides.

Size: Macaronis weigh 10 pounds and are a little over 2 feet tall.

Fun Fact: They have funny hair! Macaroni penguins are known for their black faces and the orange-yellow crests that create a band across their foreheads.

Macaroni Penguin

Little-blue Penguins

by Tim

Little-blue penguins live off the coasts of Australia and New Zealand. As their name suggests, their gray feathers look more blue in sunlight.

Size: Little-blue Penguins are only 2 pounds and 10 inches tall!

Fun Fact: Little-blue Penguins live in sandy burrows at night and go to the ocean during the day. In Australia, there is an annual "Penguin Parade" where tourists set up lights and watch the penguins return to their homes at dusk!

Little-blue Penguin

Gentoo Penguins

by Wanda

Gentoo penguins are the most far-ranging penguin species. Gentoos have a wide, white stripe across the top of their heads that looks like a bonnet. Gentoos make circular nests out of stones, and the parents take turns sitting on the eggs. When the youngsters are about three-quarters grown, they join other young penguins in large groups to look after themselves.

Size: Gentoos are 13 pounds and 32 inches tall.

Fun Fact: Some gentoos have bright red eyes.

Gentoo Penguin

Join my class on all of our Magic School Bus adventures!